HORRID HENRY'S
STINK BOMB

Meet HORRID HENRY
the laugh-out-loud worldwide sensation!

....

★ Over 15 million copies sold in 27 countries and counting

★ #1 chapter book series in the UK

★ Francesca Simon is the only American author to ever win the Galaxy British Book Awards Children's Book of the year (past winners include J.K. Rowling, Philip Pullman, and Eoin Colfer).

"Horrid Henry is a fabulous antihero…**a modern comic classic**." —*Guardian*

"**Wonderfully appealing to girls and boys alike**, a precious rarity at this age." —Judith Woods, *Times*

....

"The best children's comic writer."
—Amanda Craig, *The Times*

....

"**I love the Horrid Henry books by Francesca Simon**. They have lots of funny bits in. And Henry always gets into trouble!" —Mia, age 6, *BBC Learning Is Fun*

"My two boys love this book, and **I have actually had tears running down my face and had to stop reading because of laughing so hard**." —T. Franklin, Parent

"**It's easy to see why Horrid Henry is the bestselling character for five- to eight-year-olds**." —*Liverpool Echo*

"Francesca Simon's truly horrific little boy is **a monstrously enjoyable creation**. Parents love them because Henry makes their own little darlings seem like angels." —*Guardian Children's Books Supplement*

"I have tried out the Horrid Henry books with groups of children as a parent, as a babysitter, and as a teacher. **Children love to either hear them read aloud or to read them themselves**." —Danielle Hall, Teacher

"A flicker of recognition must pass through most teachers and parents when they read Horrid Henry. **There's a tiny bit of him in all of us**." —Nancy Astee, *Child Education*

"**As a teacher...it's great to get a series of books my class loves.** They go mad for Horrid Henry." —A teacher

"**Henry is a beguiling hero who has entranced millions of reluctant readers**." —*Herald*

....

"**An absolutely fantastic series and surely a winner with all children. Long live Francesca Simon and her brilliant books! More, more please!**" —A parent

....

"**Laugh-out-loud reading for both adults and children alike**." —A parent

"**Horrid Henry certainly lives up to his name, and his antics are everything you hope your own child will avoid—which is precisely why younger children so enjoy these tales**."
—*Independent on Sunday*

"Henry might be unbelievably naughty, totally wicked, and utterly horrid, but **he is frequently credited with converting the most reluctant readers into enthusiastic ones**...superb in its simplicity." —*Liverpool Echo*

"Will make you laugh out loud."

—Sunday Times

"Parents reading them aloud may be consoled to discover that Henry can always be relied upon to behave worse than any of their own offspring." —*Independent*

"**What is brilliant about the books is that Henry never does anything that is subversive**. She creates an aura of supreme naughtiness (of which children are in awe) but points out that he operates within a safe and secure world...**eminently readable** books." —Emily Turner, *Angels and Urchins*

"Inventive and funny, with appeal for boys and girls alike, and super illustrations by Tony Ross."

—Jewish Chronicle

"Accompanied by fantastic black-and-white drawings, the book is a joy to read. **Horrid Henry has an irresistible appeal to everyone—child and adult alike!** He is the child everyone is familiar with—irritating, annoying, but you still cannot help laughing when he gets into yet another scrape. Not quite a devil in disguise but you cannot help wondering at times! No wonder he is so popular!" —Angela Youngman

Horrid Henry by Francesca Simon

HORRID HENRY'S
STINK BOMB

Francesca Simon
Illustrated by Tony Ross

SOURCEBOOKS
Jabberwocky
AN IMPRINT OF SOURCEBOOKS

Published by Sourcebooks Jabberwocky, an imprint of Sourcebooks, Inc.
P.O. Box 4410, Naperville, Illinois 60567–4410
(630) 961–3900
Fax: (630) 961–2168
www.jabberwockykids.com

Originally published in Great Britain in 2002 by Orion Children's Books.

Library of Congress Cataloging-in-Publication Data

Simon, Francesca.
  Horrid Henry's stinkbomb / Francesca Simon ; illustrated by Tony Ross.
    p. cm.
  Originally published: Great Britain : Orion Children's Books, 2002.
  [1. Behavior—Fiction.] I. Ross, Tony, ill. II. Title.
  PZ7.S604Hss 2009
  [Fic]—dc22
                              2008039690

              Printed and bound in the United States of America.
              VP 10 9 8 7 6 5 4 3 2 1

For Joshua

CONTENTS

1

HORRID HENRY READS A BOOK

Blah blah blah blah blah.

Miss Battle-Axe droned on and on and on. Horrid Henry drew pictures of crocodiles munching on a juicy Battle-Axe snack in his math book.

Snap! Off went her head.

Yank! Bye-bye leg.

Crunch! Ta-ta teeth.

Yum yum. Henry's crocodile had a big fat smile on its face.

Blah blah blah books blah blah blah read blah blah blah prize blah blah

…PRIZE?

Horrid Henry stopped doodling.

"What prize?" he shrieked.

"Don't shout out, Henry," said Miss Battle-Axe.

Horrid Henry waved his hand and shouted:

"What prize?"

"Well, Henry, if you'd been paying attention instead of scribbling, you'd know, wouldn't you?" said Miss Battle-Axe.

Horrid Henry scowled. Typical teacher. You're interested enough in what they're saying to ask a question, and suddenly they don't want to answer.

"So, class, as I was saying before I was so rudely interrupted—" she glared at Horrid Henry— "you'll have two weeks to read as many books as you can for our school reading competition. Whoever reads the most books will win an exciting prize. A very exciting prize. But remember, a book report on every book on your list, please."

Oh. A reading competition. Horrid Henry slumped in his chair. Phooey. Reading was hard, heavy work. Just turning the pages made Henry feel exhausted. Why couldn't they ever do fun competitions, like whose tummy could rumble the loudest, or who shouted out the most in class, or who knew the rudest words? Horrid Henry would win *those* competitions every time.

But no. Miss Battle-Axe would never have a *fun* competition. Well, no way was he taking part in a reading contest. Henry

would just have to watch someone undeserving like Clever Clare or Brainy Brian swagger off with the prize while he sat prize-less at the back. It was so unfair!

"What's the prize?" shouted Moody Margaret.

Probably something awful like a pencil case, thought Horrid Henry. Or a bumper pack of school dish rags.

"Candy!" shouted Greedy Graham.

"A million bucks!" shouted Rude Ralph.

"Clothes!" shouted Gorgeous Gurinder.

"A skateboard!" shouted Aerobic Al.

"A hamster!" said Anxious Andrew.

"Silence!" bellowed Miss Battle-Axe. "The prize is a family ticket to a brand new theme park."

Horrid Henry sat up. A theme park! Oh wow! He loved theme parks! Roller coasters! Water rides! Cotton candy! His mean, horrible parents never took

him to theme parks. They dragged him to
museums. They hauled him on hikes. But
if he won the competition, they'd have to
take him. He had to win that prize. He
had to. But how could he win a reading
competition without reading any books?

"Do comics count?" shouted Rude
Ralph.

Horrid Henry's heart leapt.
He was king of the
comic book readers.
He'd easily win a comic
book competition.

Miss Battle-Axe
glared at Ralph with
her beady eyes.

"Of course not!" she
said. "Clare! How many
books do you think you
can read?"

"Fifteen," said Clever
Clare.

"Brian?"

"Eighteen," said Brainy Brian.

"Nineteen," said Clare.

"Twenty," said Brian.

Horrid Henry smiled. Wouldn't they get a shock when *he* won the prize? He'd start reading the second he got home.

Horrid Henry stretched out in the comfy black chair and switched on the TV. He had plenty of time to read. He'd start tomorrow.

Tuesday. Oh boy! Five new comics!

He'd read them first and start on all those books later.

Wednesday. Whoopee! A Mutant Max TV special! He'd definitely get reading afterward.

Thursday. Rude Ralph brought over his great new computer game, "Mash 'em! Smash 'em!" Henry mashed and smashed and mashed and smashed…

Friday. Yawn. Horrid Henry was exhausted after his long, hard week. I'll read tons of books tomorrow, thought Henry. After all, there was tons of time till the competition ended.

"How many books have *you* read, Henry?" asked Perfect Peter, looking up from the sofa.

"Tons," lied Henry.

"I've read five," said Perfect Peter proudly. "More than anyone in my class."

"Goody for you," said Henry.

"You're just jealous," said Peter.

"As if I'd ever be jealous of you, worm," sneered Henry. He wandered over to the sofa. "So what are you reading?"

"*The Happy Nappy*," said Peter.

The Happy Nappy! Trust Peter to read a stupid book like that.

"What's it about?" asked Henry, snorting.

"It's great," said Peter. "It's all about this diaper—" Then he stopped. "Wait, I'm not telling *you*. You just want to find out so you can use it in the competition. Well, you're too late. Tomorrow is the last day."

Horrid Henry felt as if a dagger had been plunged into his heart. This couldn't be. Tomorrow! How had tomorrow sneaked up so fast?

"What!" shrieked Henry. "The competition ends—tomorrow?"

"Yes," said Peter. "You should have

8

started reading sooner. After all, why put off till tomorrow what you can do today?"

"Shut up!" said Horrid Henry. He looked around wildly. What to do, what to do. He had to read something, anything—fast.

"Gimme that!" snarled Henry, snatching Peter's book. Frantically, he started to read:

"I'm unhappy, pappy," said the snappy nappy. "A happy nappy is a clappy—"

Perfect Peter snatched back his book.

"No!" screamed Peter, holding on tightly. "It's mine."

Henry lunged.

"Mine!"

"Mine!"

Riii—iippp.

"MOOOOMMMM!" screamed Peter. "Henry tore my book!"

Mom and Dad ran into the room.

"You're fighting—over a book?" said Mom. She sat down in a chair.

"I'm speechless," said Mom.

"Well, I'm not," said Dad. "Henry! Go to your room!"

"Fine!" screamed Horrid Henry.

Horrid Henry prowled up and down his bedroom. He had to think of something. Fast.

Aha! The room was full of books. He'd just copy down lots of titles. Phew. Easy-peasy.

And then suddenly Horrid Henry

remembered. He had to write a book report for every book he read. Rats. Miss Battle-Axe knew tons and tons of books. She was sure to know the plot of *Jack the Kangaroo* or *The Adventures of Terry the Towel*.

Well, he'd just have to borrow Peter's list.

Horrid Henry sneaked into Peter's bedroom. There was Peter's competition entry, in the center of Peter's immaculate desk. Henry read it.

Of course Peter would have the boring and horrible *Mouse Goes to Town*. Could he live with the shame of having baby books like *The Happy Nappy* and *Mouse Goes to Town* on his competition entry?

For a day at a theme park, anything.

Quickly, Henry copied Peter's list and book reports. Whoopee! Now he had five books. Wheel of Death here I come, thought Horrid Henry.

Then Henry had to face the terrible truth. Peter's books wouldn't be enough to win. He'd heard Clever Clare had seventeen. If only he didn't have to write those book reports. Why, oh why, did Miss Battle-Axe have to know every book ever written?

And then suddenly Henry had a brilliant, spectacular idea. It was so brilliant, and so simple, that Horrid Henry was amazed. Of course there were books that Miss Battle-Axe didn't know. Books that hadn't been written—yet.

Horrid Henry grabbed his list.

"*Mouse Goes to Town*. The thrilling adventures of a mouse in town. He meets a dog, a cat, and a duck."

12

Why should that poor mouse just go to town? Quickly Henry began to scribble.

"*Mouse Goes to the Country*. The thrilling adventures of a mouse in the country. He meets—"

Henry paused. What sort of things *did* you meet in the country? Henry had no idea.

Aha. Henry wrote quickly. "He meets a sheep and a werewolf."

"*Mouse Goes Around the World*. Mouse discovers that the world is round."

"*Mouse Goes to the Bathroom*. The thrilling adventures of one mouse and his potty."

Now, perhaps, something a little different. How about *A Boy and his Pig*. What could that book be about? thought Henry.

"Once upon a time there was a boy and his pig. They played together every day. The pig went oink."

Sounds good to me, thought Henry.

Then there was *A Pig and his Boy*. And, of course, *A Boyish Pig. A Piggish Boy. Two Pigs and a Boy. Two Boys and a Pig.*

Horrid Henry wrote and wrote and wrote. When he had filled up four pages with books and reports, and his hand ached from writing, he stopped and counted.

Twenty-seven books! Surely that was more than enough!

Miss Battle-Axe rose from her seat and walked to the podium in the school hall. Horrid Henry was so excited he could scarcely breathe. He had to win. He was sure to win.

"Well done, everyone," said Miss Battle-Axe. "So many wonderful books read. But sadly, there can be only one winner."

Me! thought Horrid Henry.

"The winner of the school reading competition, the winner who will be receiving a fabulous prize, is—" Horrid

Henry got ready to leap up— "Clare, with twenty-eight books!"

Horrid Henry sank back down in his seat as Clever Clare swaggered up to the podium. If only he'd added *Three Boys, Two Pigs, and a Rhinoceros* to his list, he'd have tied for first. It was so unfair. All his hard work for nothing.

"Well done, Clare!" beamed Miss Battle-Axe. She waved Clare's list. "I see you've read one of my very favorites, *Boudicca's Big Battle*."

She stopped. "Oh dear. Clare, you've put down *Boudicca's Big Battle* twice by mistake. But never mind. I'm sure no one else has read *twenty-seven* books—"

"I have!" screamed Horrid Henry. Leaping and shouting, punching the air with his fist, Horrid Henry ran up onto the stage, chanting: "Theme park! Theme park! Theme park!"

"Gimme my prize!" he screeched, snatching the tickets out of Clare's hand.

"Mine!" screamed Clare, snatching them back.

Miss Battle-Axe looked grim. She scanned Henry's list.

"I am not familiar with the *Boy and Pig* series," she said.

"That's 'cause it's Australian," said Horrid Henry.

Miss Battle-Axe glared at him. Then she tried to twist her face into a smile.

"It appears we have a tie," she said. "Therefore, you will each receive a family pass to the new theme park, Book World. Congratulations."

Horrid Henry stopped his victory dance. Book World? Book World? Surely he'd heard wrong?

"Here are just some of the wonderful attractions you will enjoy at Book World," said Miss Battle-Axe. "'Thrill to a display of speed-reading! Practice checking out library books! Read to the beat!' Oh my, doesn't that sound fun!"

"AAAAAARGGGGGGGGG!" screamed Horrid Henry.

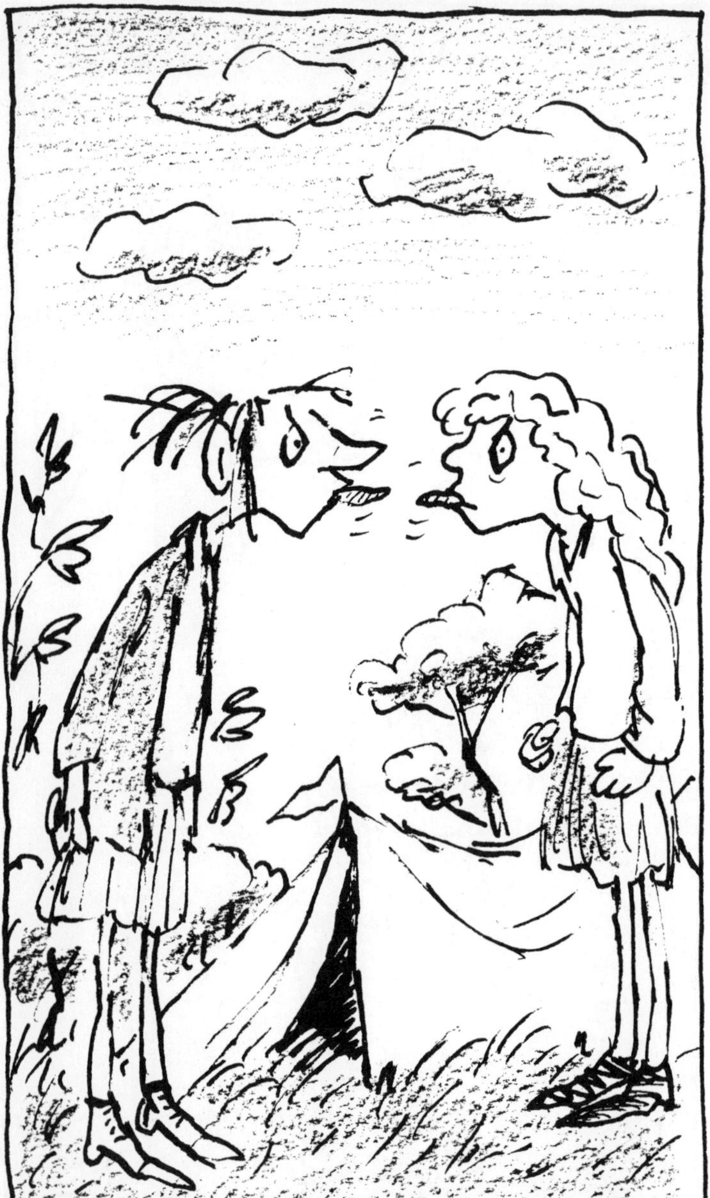

2

HORRID HENRY'S STINKBOMB

"I hate you, Margaret!" shrieked Sour Susan. She stumbled out of the Secret Club tent.

"I hate you too!" shrieked Moody Margaret.

Sour Susan stuck out her tongue.

Moody Margaret stuck out hers back.

"I quit!" yelled Susan.

"You can't quit. You're fired!" yelled Margaret.

"You can't fire me. I quit!" said Susan.

"I fired you first," said Margaret. "And I'm changing the password!"

"Go ahead. See if I care. I don't want

to be in the Secret Club any more!"
said Susan sourly.

"Good! Because *we* don't want you."

Moody Margaret flounced back inside
the Secret Club tent. Sour Susan stalked
off.

Free at last! Susan was sick and
tired of her ex-best friend Bossyboots
Margaret. Blaming *her* for the disastrous
raid on the Purple Hand Fort when it
was all Margaret's fault was bad enough.
But then to ask stupid Linda to join the
Secret Club without even telling her!
Susan hated Linda even more than she
hated Margaret. Linda hadn't invited
Susan to her sleepover party. And she
was a copycat. But Margaret didn't care.
Today she'd made Linda chief spy. Well,
Susan had had enough. Margaret had
been mean to her once too often.

Susan heard roars of laughter from inside
the club tent. So they were laughing, were

they? Laughing at her, no doubt? Well, she'd show them. She knew all about Margaret's Top Secret Plans. And she knew someone who would be very interested in that information.

"Halt! Password!"

"Smelly toads," said Perfect Peter. He waited outside Henry's Purple Hand Fort.

"Wrong," said Horrid Henry.

"What's the new one then?" said Perfect Peter.

"I'm not telling *you*," said Henry. "You're fired, remember?"

Perfect Peter did remember. He had hoped Henry had forgotten.

"Can't I join again, Henry?" asked Peter.

"No way!" said Horrid Henry.

"Please?" said Perfect Peter.

"No," said Horrid Henry. "Ralph's taken over your duties."

Rude Ralph poked his head through the branches of Henry's lair.

"No babies allowed," said Rude Ralph.

"We don't want you here, Peter," said Horrid Henry. "Get lost."

Perfect Peter burst into tears.

"Crybaby!" jeered Horrid Henry.

"Crybaby!" jeered Rude Ralph.

That did it.

"Mom!" wailed Perfect Peter. He ran toward the house. "Henry won't let me play and he called me a crybaby!"

"Stop being horrid, Henry!" shouted Mom.

Peter waited.

Mom didn't say anything else.

Perfect Peter started to wail louder.

"Mooom! Henry's being mean to me!"

"Leave Peter alone, Henry!" shouted Mom. She came out of the house. Her hands were covered in dough. "Henry, if you don't stop—"

Mom looked around.

"Where's Henry?"

"In his fort," sniveled Peter.

"I thought you said he was being mean to you," said Mom.

"He was!" wailed Peter.

"Just keep away from him," said Mom. She went back into the house.

Perfect Peter was outraged. Was that it? Why hadn't she pun-ished Henry? Henry had been so horrid he deserved to go to prison for a year. Two years. And just get a crust of bread a week. And brussels sprouts. Ha! That would serve Henry right.

25

But until Henry went to prison, how could Peter pay him back?

And then Peter knew exactly what he could do.

He checked carefully to see that no one was watching. Then he sneaked over the garden wall and headed for the Secret Club Tent.

"He isn't!" said Margaret.

"She wouldn't," said Henry.

"He's planning to swap our lemonade for a Dungeon Drink?" said Margaret.

26

"Yes," said Peter.

"She's planning to stinkbomb the Purple Hand Fort?" said Henry.

"Yes," said Susan.

"How dare she?" said Henry.

"How dare he?" said Margaret. "I'll easily put a stop to that. Linda!" she barked. "Hide the lemonade!"

Linda yawned.

"Hide it yourself," she said. "I'm tired."

Margaret glared at her, then hid the jug under a box.

"Ha ha! Won't Henry be shocked

27

when he sneaks over and there are no drinks to spike!" gloated Margaret. "Peter, you're a hero. I award you the Triple Star, the highest honor the Secret Club can bestow."

"Ooh, thanks!" said Peter. It was nice being appreciated for a change.

"So from now on," said Moody Margaret, "you're working for me."

"Okay," said the traitor.

Horrid Henry rubbed his hands. This was fantastic! At last, he had a spy in the enemy's camp! He'd easily

defend himself against that stupid stinkbomb. Margaret would only let it off when he was *in* the fort. His sentry would be on the lookout armed with a goo-shooter. When Margaret tried to sneak in with her stinkbomb— ker-pow!

"Hang on a sec," said Horrid Henry, "why should I trust you?"

28

"Because Margaret is mean and horrible and I hate her," said Susan.

"So from now on," said Horrid Henry, "you're working for me."

Susan wasn't sure she liked the sound of that. Then she remembered Margaret's mean cackle.

"Okay," said the traitor.

Peter sneaked back into his garden and collided with someone.

"Ouch!" said Peter.

"Watch where you're going!" snapped Susan.

29

They glared at each other suspiciously.

"What were you doing at Margaret's?" said Susan.

"Nothing," said Peter. "What were you doing at my house?"

"Nothing," said Susan.

Peter walked toward Henry's fort, whistling.

Susan walked toward Margaret's tent, whistling.

Well, if Susan was spying on Henry for Margaret, Peter certainly wasn't going to warn him. Serve Henry right.

Well, if Peter was spying on Margaret for Henry, Susan certainly wasn't going to warn her. Serve Margaret right.

Dungeon Drinks, eh?

Margaret liked that idea much better than her stinkbomb plot.

"I've changed my mind about the stinkbomb," said Margaret. "I'm going to swap his drinks for Dungeon Drink stinkers instead."

"Good idea," said Lazy Linda. "Less work."

Stinkbomb, eh?

Henry liked that much better than his Dungeon Drink plot. Why hadn't he thought of that himself?

"I've changed my mind about the Dungeon Drinks," said Henry. "I'm going to stinkbomb her instead."

"Yeah," said Rude Ralph. "When?"

"Now," said Horrid Henry. "Come on, let's go to my room."

Horrid Henry opened his Stinky Stinkbomb kit. He'd bought it with Grandma. Mom would *never* have let him buy it. But because Grandma had given him the money Mom couldn't do anything about it. Ha ha ha.

Now, which stink would he pick?
He looked at the test tubes filled with
powder and read the gruesome labels.

Bad breath. Dog poo. Rotten eggs.
Smelly socks. Dead fish. Sewer stench.

"I'd go for dead fish," said Ralph.
"That's the worst."

Henry considered.

"How about we mix dead fish *and*
rotten eggs?"

"Yeah," said Rude Ralph.

Slowly, carefully, Horrid Henry
measured out a teaspoon of dead fish
powder, and a teaspoon of rotten egg
powder, into the special pouch.

Slowly, carefully, Rude Ralph poured out 150 milliliters of secret stinkbomb liquid into the bottle and capped it tightly.

All they had to do was to add the powder to the bottle outside the Secret Club— and run!

"Ready?" said Horrid Henry.

"Ready," said Rude Ralph.

"Whatever you do," said Horrid Henry, "don't spill it."

"So you've come crawling back," said Moody Margaret. "I knew you would."

"No," said Sour Susan. "I just happened to be passing."

She looked around the Secret Club
Tent.

"Where's Linda?"

Margaret scowled. "Gone."

"Gone for today, or gone forever?" said
Susan.

"Forever," said Margaret savagely. "I
don't ever want to see that lazy lump
again."

Margaret and Susan looked at each
other.

Susan tapped her foot.

Margaret hummed.

"Well?" said Margaret.

"Well what?" said Susan.

"Are you rejoining the Secret Club as
Chief Spy or aren't you?"

"I might," said Susan. "And I might not."

"Suit yourself," said Margaret. "I'll call
Gurinder and ask her to join instead."

"Okay," said Susan quickly. "I'll join."

34

Should she mention her visit to
Henry? Better not. After all, what
Margaret didn't know wouldn't hurt her.

"Now, about my stinkbomb plot,"
began Margaret. "I decided—"

Something shattered on the ground
inside the tent. A ghastly, gruesome,
grisly stinky stench filled the air.

"AAAAARGGGGG!" screamed
Margaret, gagging. "It's a—
STINKBOMB!"

"HELP!" shrieked Sour Susan.
"STINKBOMB! Help! Help!"

Victory! Horrid Henry and Rude Ralph ran back to the Purple Hand Fort and rolled around the floor, laughing and shrieking.

What a triumph!

Margaret and Susan screaming! Margaret's mom screaming! Margaret's dad screaming! And the stink! Wow! Horrid Henry had never smelled anything so awful in his life.

This called for a celebration.

Horrid Henry offered Ralph a fistful of candy and poured out two glasses of Fizzywizz drinks.

"Cheers!" said Henry.

"Cheers!" said Ralph.

They drank.

"AAAAAARRGGGGGG!" choked Rude Ralph.

"Blecccccch!" yelped Horrid Henry, gagging and spitting. "We've been—" cough!— "Dungeon-Drinked!"

And then Horrid Henry heard a horrible sound. Moody Margaret and Sour Susan were outside the Purple Hand Fort. Chanting a victory chant:

"NAH NAH NE NAH NAH!"

3

HORRID HENRY'S SCHOOL PROJECT

"Susan! Stop shouting!

Ralph! Stop running!

William! Stop weeping!

Henry! Just stop!"

Miss Battle-Axe glared at her class. Her class glared back.

"Miss!" screeched Lazy Linda. "Henry's pulling my hair."

"Miss!" screeched Gorgeous Gurinder. "Ralph's kicking me."

"Miss!" screeched Anxious Andrew. "Dave's poking me."

"Stop it, Henry!" barked Miss Battle-Axe.

Henry stopped. What was bothering the old bat now?

"Class, pay attention," said Miss Battle-Axe. "Today we're doing Group Projects on the Ancient Greeks. We're studying—"

"—the sacking of Troy!" shrieked Henry. Yes! He could see it now. Henry, leading the Greeks as they crashed and slashed their way through the terrified Trojans. His spear would be the longest, and the sharpest, and—

Miss Battle-Axe fixed Henry with her icy stare. Henry froze.

"We're going to divide into small groups and make Parthenons out of cardboard toilet paper rolls and construction paper," continued Miss Battle-Axe. "First you must draw the Parthenon, agree on a design together, then build and paint it. I want to see *everyone* sharing and listening. "Also, the Principal will be dropping by to admire your work and to see how beautifully you are working together."

Horrid Henry scowled. He hated working in groups. He detested sharing. He loathed listening to others. Their ideas were always wrong. His ideas were always right. But the other children in Henry's groups never recognized Henry's genius. For some reason they wanted to do things *their* way, not his.

The Ancient Greeks certainly never worked together beautifully, thought Horrid Henry resentfully, so why should he? They just speared each other or ate their children for dinner.

"Henry, Bert, William, and Clare, you're working together on Table Three," said Miss Battle-Axe.

Horrid Henry groaned. What a horrible, horrible group. He hated all of them. Why didn't Miss Battle-Axe ever put him in a fun group, with Ralph or Graham or Dave? Henry could see it now. They'd be laughing together in the corner, making

41

trumpets out of toilet paper rolls, sneaking candy, throwing crayons, flicking paint, having a great time.

But oh no. He had to be with bossy-boots Clare, crybaby William and—Bert. Miss Battle-Axe did it on purpose, just to torture him.

"NO!" protested Horrid Henry. "I can't work with *her!*"

"NO!" protested Clever Clare. "I can't work with *him!*"

"Waaaaah," wailed Weepy William. "I want to work with Andrew."

"Silence!" shouted Miss Battle-Axe. "Now get in your groups and get to work. I want to see everyone sharing and working together beautifully—or else."

There was a mad scramble as everyone ran to their tables to grab the best pencils and the most pieces of paper.

Henry snatched the purple, blue, and red pencils and a big pile of paper.

"I haven't got any paper!" screamed William.

"Tough," said Horrid Henry. "I need all these for my design."

"I want some paper!" whined William.

Clever Clare passed him one of her sheets.

43

William burst into tears.

"It's dirty," he wailed. "And I haven't got a pencil."

"Here's what we're going to do," said Henry. "I'm doing the design, William can help me build it, and everyone can watch me paint."

"No way, Henry," said Clare. "We *all* do a design, then we make the best one."

"Which will be mine," said Horrid Henry.

"Doubt it," said Clever Clare.

"Well I'm not making *yours*," snarled Henry. "And *I'm* doing the painting."

"You're doing the gluing, *I'm* doing the painting," said Clare.

"I want to do the painting," wailed William.

"What do you want to do, Bert?" asked Clare.

"I dunno," said Beefy Bert.

"Fine," said Clever Clare. "Bert will do the cleaning. Let's get drawing, everyone. We want our group's Parthenon to be the best."

Horrid Henry was outraged.

"Who made you boss?" demanded Henry.

"Someone has to take charge," said Clever Clare.

Horrid Henry reached under the table and kicked her.

"OOWWWW!" yelped Clever Clare. "Miss! Henry kicked me!"

"Did not!" shouted Horrid Henry. "Liar."

"Why isn't Table Three drawing?" hissed Miss Battle-Axe.

Clare drew.

William drew.

Bert drew.

Henry drew.

"Everyone should have finished drawing by now," said Miss Battle-Axe, patrolling among the tables. "Time to combine your ideas."

"But I haven't finished," wept William.

Horrid Henry gazed at his design with satisfaction. It was a triumph. He could see it now, painted silver and purple, with a few red stripes.

"Why don't we just build mine?" said Clare.

"'Cause mine's the best!" shouted Horrid Henry.

"What about mine?" whispered William.

"We're building mine!" shouted Clare.

"MINE!"

"MINE!"

Miss Battle-Axe ran over.

"Stop shouting!" shouted Miss Battle-Axe. "Show me your work. That's lovely, Clare. What a fabulous design."

"Thank you, Miss," said Clever Clare.

"William! That's a tower, not a temple! Start again!"

"Waaaah!" wailed William.

"Bert! What is this mess?"

"I dunno," said Beefy Bert.

"It looks like a teepee, not a temple," said Miss Battle-Axe.

She looked at Horrid Henry's design and glared at him.

"Can't you follow instructions?" she shrieked. "That temple looks like it's about to blast off."

"That's how I meant it to look," said Henry. "It's high-tech."

"Margaret! Sit down! Toby! Leave Brian alone! Graham! Get back to work," said Miss Battle-Axe, racing off to stop the fight at Table Two.

"Okay, we're doing *my* design," said Clare. "Who wants to build the steps and who wants to decorate the columns?"

"No one," snapped Horrid Henry, "'cause we're doing *mine*."

"Fine, we'll vote," said Clare. "Who wants to build mine?"

Clare and William raised their hands.

"I'll get you for that, William," muttered Henry.

William burst into tears.

"Who wants to do Henry's?" said Clare.

Only Henry raised his hand.

"Come on, Bert, don't you want to make mine?" pleaded Henry.

"I dunno," said Beefy Bert.

"It's not fair!" shrieked Horrid Henry. "I WANT TO BUILD MINE!"

"MINE!"

"MINE!"

SLAP!

SLAP!

"That's it!" shrieked Miss Battle-Axe. "Henry! Work in the corner on your own."

YES! This was the best news Henry had heard all morning.

Beaming, Henry went to the corner and sat down at his own little table, with his own glue, his own scissors, his own paints, his own construction paper, and his own pile of toilet paper rolls.

Bliss, thought Henry. I can build my Parthenon in peace.

There was just one problem. There was only a small number of toilet paper rolls left.

This isn't nearly enough for my Parthenon, thought Horrid Henry. I need more.

He went over to Moody Margaret's table.

"I need more rolls," he said.

"Tough," said Margaret. "We're using all of ours."

Henry stomped over to Sour Susan's table.

"Give me some rolls," he said.

"Go away," said Susan sourly.
"Margaret took our extras."

"Sit down, Henry," barked Miss
Battle-Axe.

Henry sat, fuming. This was an
outrage. Hadn't Miss Battle-Axe told
them to share? And here were his greedy
classmates hogging all the toilet paper
rolls when his Parthenon desperately
needed extra engines.

BUZZZ. Break time!

"Leave your Parthenons on the tables to dry," said Miss Battle-Axe. "Henry, you will stay in at break and finish."

What?

Miss break?

"But—but—"

"Sit down," ordered Miss Battle-Axe. "Or you'll go straight to the Principal's Office!"

Eeeek! Horrid Henry knew the Principal, Mrs. Oddbod, all too well. He did not need to know her any better.

Henry slunk back to his chair. Everyone else ran shrieking out of the door to the playground. Why was it always children who were punished? Why weren't teachers ever sent to the Principal's Office? It was so unfair!

"I just have to run down the hall for a moment. Don't you dare leave that table," said Miss Battle-Axe.

The moment Miss Battle-Axe left the room, Henry jumped up and accidentally on purpose knocked over Clare's chair. He broke William's pencil and drew a skull and crossbones on Bert's teepee.

Then he wandered over to Sour Susan's table. There was a freshly glued Parthenon, waiting to be painted.

Henry studied it.

You know, he thought, Susan's group hasn't done a bad job. Not bad at all. Shame about that bulge on the side, though. If they shared one roll with me, it would balance so much better.

Horrid Henry looked to the left.

He looked to the right.

Snatch! Susan's supports sagged.

Better even that up, thought Horrid Henry.

Yank!

Hmmm, thought Horrid Henry, glancing at Gurinder's table. What were they thinking? Those walls are far too tall.

Grab! Gurinder's temple tottered.

And as for Clare's pathetic efforts, it was positively bursting with useless pillars.

Whisk! Clare's columns wobbled.

Much better, thought Horrid Henry. Soon he had plenty of rolls.

CLOMP

CLOMP

CLOMP

Horrid Henry dashed back to his table and was

innocently gluing away as the class stampeded back to their tables.

Wobble

Wobble

Wobble—CRASH!

On every table, Parthenons started collapsing.

Everyone shrieked and screamed and sobbed.

"It's your fault!"

"Yours!"

"You didn't glue it right!"

"You didn't build it right!"

Rude Ralph hurled a paintbrush at Moody Margaret. Margaret hurled it back. Suddenly the room was filled with flying brushes, gluepots, and rolls.

Miss Battle-Axe burst in.

"STOP IT!" bellowed Miss Battle-Axe, as a roll hit her on the nose. "YOU ARE THE WORST CLASS I HAVE EVER TAUGHT! I LEAVE YOU ALONE FOR ONE MINUTE AND JUST LOOK AT THIS MESS! NOW SIT DOWN AND SHUT—"

The door opened. In walked the Principal.

Mrs. Oddbod stared at Miss Battle-Axe.

Miss Battle-Axe stared at Mrs. Oddbod.

"Boudicca!" said Mrs. Oddbod. "What-is-going-on?"

"The sacking of Troy!" shrieked Horrid Henry.

There was a terrible silence.

Horrid Henry shrank in his seat. Now he was done for. Now he was dead.

"I can see that," said Mrs. Oddbod coldly. "Miss Battle-Axe! Come to my office—now!"

"No!" whimpered Miss Battle-Axe.

YES! thought Horrid Henry.

Victory!

4

HORRID HENRY'S
SLEEPOVER

Horrid Henry loved sleepovers.
Midnight feasts! Pillow fights! Screaming
and shouting! Rampaging till dawn!

The time he ate all the ice cream at
Greedy Graham's and left the freezer
door open! The time he jumped on all
the beds at Dizzy Dave's and broke them
all. And that time at Rude Ralph's when
he—well, hmmm, perhaps better not
mention that.

There was just one problem. No one
would ever have Horrid Henry at their
house for a sleepover more than once.
Whenever Henry went to sleep at a
friend's house, Mom and Dad were sure

to get a call at three
a.m. from a demented
parent screaming at
them to pick up Henry
immediately.

Horrid Henry
couldn't understand it.
Parents were so fussy.
Even the parents of
great kids like Rude
Ralph and Greedy Graham. Who cares
about a little noise? Or a broken bed? Big
deal, thought Horrid Henry.

It was no fun having friends sleep
over at *his* house. There was no
rampaging and feasting at Henry's. It
was lights out as usual at nine o'clock,
no talking, no feasting, no fun.

So when New Nick, who had just
joined Henry's class, invited Henry to
stay the night, Horrid Henry couldn't
believe his luck. New beds to bounce on.

New cookie jars to raid. New places to rampage. Bliss!

Henry packed his sleepover bag as fast as he could.

Mom came in. She looked grumpy.

"Got your pajamas?" she asked.

Henry never needed pajamas at sleepovers because he never went to bed.

"Got them," said Henry. Just not *with* him, he thought.

"Don't forget your toothbrush," said Mom.

"I won't," said Horrid Henry. He never *forgot* his toothbrush—he just chose not to bring it.

Dad came in. He looked even grumpier.

"Don't forget your comb," said Dad.

Horrid Henry looked at his bulging backpack stuffed with toys and comics. Sadly, there was no room for a comb.

"I won't," lied Henry.

"I'm warning you, Henry," said Mom. "I want you to be on best behavior tonight."

"Of course," said Horrid Henry.

"I don't want any phone calls at three a.m. from Nick's parents," said Dad. "If I do, this will be your last sleepover ever. I mean it."

Nag nag nag.

"All right," said Horrid Henry.

Ding Dong.

WOOF WOOF WOOF WOOF WOOF!

A woman opened the door. She was wearing a Viking helmet on her head and long flowing robes. Behind her stood a man in a velvet cloak holding back five enormous, snarling black dogs.

"TRA LA LA BOOM-DY AY," boomed a dreadful, earsplitting voice.

"Bravo, Bravo!" shouted a chorus from the sitting room.

GRRRRRRR! growled the dogs.

Horrid Henry hesitated. Did he have the right house? Was New Nick an alien?

"Oh don't mind us, dear, it's our opera club's karaoke night," trilled the Viking helmet.

"Nick!" bellowed the Cloak. "Your friend is here."

Nick appeared. Henry was glad to see he was not wearing a Viking helmet or a velvet cloak.

"Hi Henry," said New Nick.

"Hi Nick," said Horrid Henry.

A little girl toddled over, sucking her thumb.

"Henry, this is my sister, Lily," said Nick.

Lily gazed at Horrid Henry.

"I love you, Henwy," said Lisping Lily. "Will you marry with me?"

"NO!" said Horrid Henry. Uggh.
What a revolting thought.

"Go away, Lily," said Nick.

Lily did not move.

"Come on, Nick, let's get out of here,"
said Henry. No toddler was going to spoil
his fun. Now, what would he do first, raid
the kitchen or bounce on the beds?

"Let's raid the kitchen," said Henry.

"Great," said Nick.

"Got any good candy?" asked Henry.

"Tons!" said New Nick.

Yeah! thought Horrid Henry. His sleepover fun was beginning!

They sneaked into the kitchen. The floor was covered with dog blankets, overturned food bowls, clumps of dog hair, and gnawed dog bones. There were a few suspicious looking puddles. Henry hoped they were water.

"Here are the cookies," said Nick.

Henry looked. Were those dog hairs all over the jar?

"Uh, no thanks," said Henry. "How about some candy?"

"Sure," said Nick. "Help yourself."

He handed Henry a bar of chocolate. Yummy! Henry was about to take a big

bite when he stopped. Were those—
teeth marks in the corner?

"RAAA!" A big black shape jumped
on Henry, knocked him down, and
snatched the chocolate.

Nick's dad burst in.

"Rigoletto! Give that back!" said Nick's dad, yanking the chocolate out of the dog's mouth.

"Sorry about that, Henry," he said, offering it back to Henry.

"Uhh, maybe later," said Henry.

"Okay," said Nick's dad, putting the slobbery chocolate back in the cabinet.

Eeew, gross, thought Horrid Henry.

"I love you, Henwy," came a lisping voice behind him.

"AH HA HA HA HA HA HA HA!" warbled a high, piercing voice from the sitting room.

Henry held his ears. Would the windows shatter?

"Encore!" shrieked the opera karaoke club.

"Will you marry with me?" asked Lisping Lily.

"Let's get out of here," said Horrid Henry.

Horrid Henry leapt on Nick's bed.

Yippee, thought Horrid Henry. Time to get bouncing.

Bounce—

Crash!

The bed collapsed in a heap.

"What happened?" said Henry. "I hardly did anything."

"Oh, I broke the bed ages ago," said Nick. "Dad said he was tired of fixing it."

Rats, thought Henry. What a lazy dad.

"How about a pillow fight?" said Henry.

"No pillows," said Nick. "The dogs chewed them."

Hmmm.

They *could* sneak down and raid the freezer, but for some reason Henry didn't really want to go back into that kitchen.

"I know!" said Henry. "Let's watch TV."

"Sure," said New Nick.

"Where is the TV?" said Henry.

"In the living room," said Nick.

"But—the karaoke," said Henry.

"Oh, they won't mind," said Nick. "They're used to noise in this house."

"DUM DUM DE DUM DUMM DUMM

DUM DE DUM DUMM DUMM–"

Horrid Henry sat with his face pressed to the TV. He couldn't hear a word Mutant Max was shrieking with all that racket in the background.

"Maybe we should go to bed," said Horrid Henry, sighing. Anything to get away from the noise.

"Okay," said New Nick.

Phew, thought Horrid Henry. Peace at last.

★ ★ ★

SNORE! SNORE!

Horrid Henry turned over in his sleeping bag and tried to get comfortable. He hated sleeping on the floor. He hated sleeping with the window open. He hated sleeping with the radio on.

And he hated sleeping in the same room
with someone who snored.

Awhooooooo! howled the winter
wind through the open window.

SNORE! SNORE!

"I'm just a lonesome cowboy, lookin'
for a lonesome cowgirl," blared the radio.

WOOF WOOF WOOF barked the
dogs.

"Yeowwww!" squealed Henry, as five
wet, smelly dogs pounced on him.

"Awhoooo!" howled the wind.

SNORE! SNORE!

"TOREADOR—on guard!" boomed the opera karaoke downstairs.

Horrid Henry loved noise. But this was—too much.

He'd have to find somewhere else to sleep.

Horrid Henry flung open the bedroom door.

"I love you Henwy," said Lisping Lily.

Slam! Horrid Henry shut the bedroom door.

Horrid Henry did not move.

Horrid Henry did not breathe.

Then he opened the door a fraction.

"Will you marry with me, Henwy?"

Aaarrrgh!!!

Horrid Henry ran from the bedroom and barricaded himself in the linen closet. He settled down on a pile of towels.

Phew. Safe at last.

"I want to give you a big kiss, Henwy," came a little voice beside him.

NOOOOOOOO!

It was three a.m.

"TRA LA LA BOOM-DY AY!"

"—LONESOME COWBOY!"

SNORE! SNORE!

AWHOOOOOOOOOOOOOO!

WOOF! WOOF! WOOF!

Horrid Henry crept to the hall phone and dialed his number.

Dad answered.

"I'm so sorry about Henry, do you want us to come and get him?" Dad mumbled.

"Yes," wailed Horrid Henry. "I need my rest!"

And now for a sneak peek at one of the
laugh-out-loud stories in
Horrid Henry and the Mummy's Curse

HORRID HENRY'S HOBBY

"Out of my way, worm!" shrieked Horrid Henry, pushing past his younger brother Perfect Peter and dashing into the kitchen.

"NO!" screamed Perfect Peter. He scrambled after Henry and clutched his leg.

"Get off me!" shouted Henry. He grabbed the unopened Sweet Tweet cereal box. "Nah nah ne nah nah, I got it first."

Perfect Peter lunged for the Sweet Tweet box and snatched it from Henry. "But it's my turn!"

"No, mine!" shrieked Henry.

He ripped open the top and stuck his hand inside.

"It's mine!" shrieked Peter. He ripped open the bottom.

A small wrapped toy fell to the floor.

Henry and Peter both lunged for it.

"Gimme that!" yelled Henry.

"But it's my turn to have it!" yelled Peter.

"Stop being horrid, Henry!" shouted Mom. "Now give me that thing!"

Henry and Peter both held on tight.

"NO!" screamed Henry and Peter. "IT'S MY TURN TO HAVE THE TOY!"

Horrid Henry and Perfect Peter both collected Gizmos from inside Sweet Tweet cereal boxes. So did everyone at their school. There were ten different colored Gizmos to collect, from the common green to the rare gold. Both Henry and Peter had Gizmos of every color. Except for one. Gold.

"Right," said Mom, "whose turn is it to get the toy?"

"MINE!" screamed Henry and Peter.

"He got the last one!" screeched Henry. "Remember—he opened the new box and got the blue Gizmo."

It was true that Perfect Peter had got the blue Gizmo—two boxes ago. But why should Peter get any? If he hadn't started collecting Gizmos to copy me, thought Henry resentfully, I'd get every single one.

"NO!" howled Peter. He burst into tears. "Henry opened the last box."

"Crybaby," jeered Henry.

"Stop it," said Peter.

"Stop it," mimicked Henry.

"Mom, Henry's teasing me," wailed Peter.

"I remember now," said Mom. "It's Peter's turn."

"Thank you, Mom," said Perfect Peter.

"It's not fair!" screamed Horrid Henry as Peter tore open the wrapping. There was a gold gleam.

"Oh my goodness," gasped Peter. "A gold Gizmo!"

Horrid Henry felt as if he'd been punched in the stomach. He stared at the glorious, glowing, golden Gizmo.

"It's not fair!" howled Henry. "I want a gold Gizmo!"

"I'm sorry, Henry," said Mom. "It'll be your turn next."

"But I want the gold one!" screamed Henry.

He leaped on Peter and yanked

the Gizmo out of his hand. He was
Hurricane Henry uprooting everything
in his path.

"Helllllllllp!" howled Peter.

"Stop being horrid, Henry, or no
more Gizmos for you!" shouted Mom.
"Now clean up this mess and get
dressed."

"NO!" howled Henry. He ran
upstairs to his room, slamming the door
behind him.

He had to have a gold Gizmo. He

simply had to. No one at school had a gold one. Henry could see himself now, the center of attention, everyone pushing and shoving just to get a look at his gold Gizmo. Henry could charge 50 cents a peek. Everyone would want to see it and to hold it. Henry would be invited to every birthday party. Instead, Peter would be the star attraction. Henry gnashed his teeth just thinking about it.

But how could he get one? You couldn't buy Gizmos. You could only get them inside Sweet Tweet cereal boxes. Mom was so mean she made Henry and Peter finish the old box before she'd buy a new one. Henry had eaten mountains of Sweet Tweet cereal to collect all his Gizmos. All that hard work would be in vain, unless he got a gold one.

He could, of course, steal Peter's. But Peter would be sure to notice, and

Henry would be the chief suspect.

He could swap. Yes! He would offer Peter *two* greens! That was generous. In fact, that was really generous. But Peter hated doing swaps. For some reason he always thought Henry was trying to cheat him.

And then suddenly Henry had a brilliant, spectacular idea. True, it did involve a little tiny teensy weensy bit of trickery, but Henry's cause was just. *He'd* been collecting Gizmos far longer than Peter had. He deserved a gold one, and Peter didn't.

"So, you got a gold Gizmo," said Henry, popping into Peter's room. "I'm really sorry."

Perfect Peter looked up from polishing his Gizmos. "Why?" he said suspiciously. "*Everyone* wants a gold Gizmo."

Horrid Henry looked sadly at Perfect Peter. "Not any more. They're very unlucky, you know. Every single person who's got one has died horribly."

Perfect Peter stared at Henry, then at his golden Gizmo.

"That's not true, Henry."

"Yes it is."

"No it isn't."

Horrid Henry walked slowly around Peter's room. Every so often he made a little note in a notebook.

"Marbles, check. Three knights, check. Nature kit—nah. Coin collection, check."

"What are you doing?" said Peter.

"Just looking at your stuff to see what I want when you're gone."

"Stop it!" said Peter. "You just made that up about gold Gizmos—didn't you?"

"No," said Henry. "It's in all the newspapers. There was the boy out walking his dog who fell into a pit of molten lava.

There was the girl who drowned in the toilet, and then that poor boy who—"

"I don't want to die," said Perfect Peter. He looked pale. "What am I going to do?"

Henry paused. "There's nothing you can do. Once you've got it you're sunk."

Can Henry convince Peter to give up his golden Gizmo? Will Henry get away with this dastardly plot? Find out what happens in Horrid Henry's next book: *Horrid Henry and the Mummy's Curse!*

The HORRID HENRY books
by Francesca Simon

Illustrated by Tony Ross
Each book contains four stories

HORRID HENRY

Henry is dragged to dancing class against his will; vies with Moody Margaret to make the yuckiest Glop; goes camping; and tries to be good like Perfect Peter—but not for long.

HORRiD HENRY TRiCKs THE TOOTH FAiRY

Horrid Henry tries to trick the Tooth Fairy into giving him more money; sends Moody Margaret packing; causes his teachers to run screaming from school; and single-handedly wrecks a wedding.

HORRiD HENRY and THE MEGA-MEAN TiME MACHiNE

Horrid Henry reluctantly goes for a hike; builds a time machine and convinces Perfect Peter that boys wear dresses in the future; Perfect Peter plays one of the worst tricks ever on his brother; and Henry's aunt takes the family to a fancy restaurant, so his parents bribe him to behave.

HORRID HENRY AND THE MUMMY'S CURSE

Horrid Henry indulges his favorite hobby—collecting Gizmos; has a bad time with his spelling homework; starts a rumor that there's a shark in the pool; and spooks Perfect Peter with the mummy's curse.

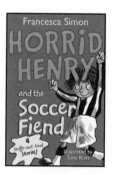

Francesca Simon

HORRID HENRY AND THE SOCCER FIEND

Horrid Henry reads Perfect Peter's diary and improves it; goes shopping with Mom and tries to make her buy him some really nice new sneakers; is horrified when his old enemy Bossy Bill turns up at school; and tries by any means, to win the class soccer match.

About the Author

Photo: Francesco Guidicini

Francesca Simon spent her childhood on the beach in California and then went to Yale and Oxford Universities to study medieval history and literature. She now lives in London with her family. She has written over forty-five books and won the Children's Book of the Year in 2008 at the Galaxy British Book Awards for *Horrid Henry and the Abominable Snowman*.